# Echo

Journey Johnson

Echo

To my beloved Echo
Thank you for your patience with me.
Welcome to the world.

# CONTENTS

| VI | —

# Echo: The Beautiful Ugly

**by Journey Johnson**

VERBANIZM | **INK**

Copyright © 2024 by **Journey Johnson**



**Echo: The Beautiful Ugly| Journey Johnson**. -- 1st ed.
ISBN 978-0-09899300-1-7

In a mad world, only the mad are sane.
Akira Kuroawa

## One

# Covenant

As it was
She had never been told
She was beautiful.

It was kept on the hush
Like a secret that would unchain
The world as she knew it.

And that chain was a
Thin and fraying thread.
A mother's closet.
A father's dereliction.

For what is beauty to a beast
But something to be slain.
Some *thing* left to appease the
Palettes of vultures piqued by

Pheromones of decay.

They are vampires on the hunt
For young blood. Tender flesh.
A broken home. A picket fence
A blind eye. An unlocked door.

Buzzards circle.
Forming rings of
Fiending gods.

They pluck the eyes first.
For beauty be in the optics.
They behold her.

We. opt for obscurity.
Beauty be a perilous notion.
A vacuum to a portal to vanity so waxed,
Self-esteem be a worthy sacrifice.

It is an absolute necessity
This sacrifice of self-esteem.
Confidence may lead one to believe
They are special. That they deserve

More than the scraps they
Are given. Infinitely bigger than
The tiny, yet toxic thought
Patterns that cage them.

Self-esteem be an obstacle
To they who maneuver to
Manipulate, to maim all things
Beautiful and free.

Lest the legs become loose.
Lest the ass become fast.
Lest the babies come falling,
Duplicate mouths looking
For handouts.

Hand-me-down souls
Exhausted since birth.
A blues played to
Trap music.

Lest the streets surrender
Countless more sons. Sacrifices to
Gunpowder gods. Deities
Of chaos and destruction.

Lest vast more daughters be sold
Invisible and unnamed. Offerings
To the putrid phallus of traffickers,
Dealers, pimps, priests. Family.

Lest the kindling overwhelm.
Lest the stench of blazing innocence

Prove too much for the crematorium
Burning down the suburbs
And hood, alike.

# The Process

Thus, methodically as intravenous,
She was birthed and raised in an ugly
So deep, it soiled the psyche.

There are means of actualizing self-loathing
Such that the perceived responsibility of the dysfunction
Lies solely in the mind of the sufferer.

To this end, she was slipped subliminal
Clues sprinkled casual and careless as crumbs
From the mouths of her closest relations.
Blood, bond, and otherwise.

Crumbs to be followed back to the rock
That should have crushed her at birth,
Saving those around her the trouble of
Having to chip away at her dignity

One nick, one dent,
One full-on, full-blown
Demolition at a time.

Projected code words
And catchphrases like:

Black. and Ashy. Rachet. Broke.
Ghetto. and Country. Thug. Bald
Headed. Nappy. Crispy. Blackie.
Nigger. Nigglet. Nigga.

*Do somethin' bout that hair, nigga!*

Where she's from, *Nigga*
Is the term of choice, no
Matter the ethnicity.

Hence:

*Damn, you black, nigga.*
*Big lipped nigga. Wit 'cho*
*Dick suckin' lips, nigga.*

*You need to do somethin' bout*
*Bein' so goddamn crispy, nigga. You know*
*They got bleach for that shit.*

Visceral.

Yet, ugly doesn't confine itself
To things as trife as race or complexion.
The pique is pandemic.

*What 'chu lookin' at fatty?*
*What's the matter, big 'Ems*
*Cat got your burger? Tee hee.*

Clues.
Scattered.
Casual.

*Shit, you skinny!*
*Too damned skinny. Eww*
*Your mama know you on crack?*

Careless.

*This bitch ain't got no titties.*
*That bitch got too much titties.*
*Get the fuck on wit 'cho*
*Saggin' ass titties.*

Code words.

*But, how you fat*
*And ain't got no ass? And you?*
*You ain't nothin' **but** ass, ho.*

*It's all you good for.*
*I asked your daddy*
*He thinks so, too.*

Casual.
Careless.
Coded.
Clues.

As far
As the eye
Can see.

## Three |

## Crouching Snipers

Ever want to hide a dagger?
Wrap it in laughter.
Serve it up cold.

Add a cup of 'jokes' on the side,
Hold the apologies. The method is
Foolproof. An easy slay.

Jealousy is a wily thing.
It is a dangerous thing.

*Hate* is a coward's word
When referencing someone
Who's committed no offense.

It is far easier to say-
I hate you
Than it is to say

I am jealous of you.

If a hater can't kill your spirit
They will kill your dreams
Or they will kill you.

Listen.
Are you listening?
Listen.

If a nigga got jokes
Step away from the punchline.
It's a killer.

## Four

## Lineage

To be clear,
Ugly doesn't just happen.
Un-beautifying is a process
Perfected through generations

Genuine time and effort go into
Making gruesome proper enough to carry
Weight of legitimacy in official quarters
Until the act itself is intrinsic.

It is in the slide of eye.
Ever in favor of that which is lighter
That which is whiter. They banished
Blackness with the bible.

Big noses and big lips
Are liabilities in a society
Born and bred off Eurocentricity's

Blueprint of beauty.

It seeps into the blood.
It is a pathogen promulgated by propaganda
And carried by subconscious collusion
Against the soul itself.

There is a malignance in the
Marrow of the mind.
Symptoms of the spirit
Manifest in mental mirages.

There is something in the water.
Everybody's drinking it.
Something in the air's
Got everybody thinking it.

## Five

# Familiar

One can run from all outside.
One can retreat from
The cruelty of the world

As long as that cruelty
Ends at the front door.

Inside is different.
Inside is family.
Inside is inescapable.

Within familiar walls,
Truth be told, there is
No one with whom to
Share the homeliness.

No proud legacy of awkward forefathers.
No bad built foremothers of regal bearing.

No nods of understanding between
Outcasts of shared bloodlines.

Home is where self-loathing festers.
There are no protective glares directed at mirrors
Threatening treason of misery's reflection.

No, within the family
Ugly begins and ends in the solitary
Confinement of one

And she is it.

## Six

## RSVP

In the dining room, subtle
Assaults were launched at the
Appalling intruder rude enough
To bring her face to the table where
Decent folks were trying to eat.

Rampant were the unreported
Misdemeanours bordering felonies.
*'Pass the potatoes please'*
Would start the onslaught.

**Dissolve to dinner scene:**

*-Girl, how much are you gonna eat?*
*If you chewed as slow as you look*
*You would be full by now.*

**Reverb sibling snicker into audio:**

*-You've had enough anyway.*
*Every time I turn around. I'm*
*Buying bigger clothes for you.*
*Money grows on trees now?*

*-Plus, your sister's trying out*
*For cheerleading, That'll take*
*More funds. Think about somebody*
*Besides yourself for once.*

**Zoom in on 'why can't you be like your sister' look.**
**Hold focus as exchange continues:**

-But I-

*-And wipe that look off your face*

-(she wishes she could)

*-Before I knock it off*

-(she wishes they would)

Knock it clean off. Let it fly
Off her shoulders and
On out the door.

If God is real, it will find its way

Into rush hour traffic; where a
Careening Yellow Cab will
Swerve serendipitous,
Smashing the ugly
To ashes.

**Fade back to convo:**

*-Are you listening to me?*

Of course, she is. How could she
Not, given the enormity of her ears?

They think she wraps her hair before bed.
She doesn't. She pins her ears
And swaddles the voices.

*-And didn't I tell you to stay out the sun?*
*Your ass is black enough as it is.*
*Don't let night fall on that tail.*
*Ain't nobody gonna be able to find you.*

*-And what're you cryin' for?*

She wasn't crying. Wasn't even
Thinking of crying. But the very thought
Of looking like she was crying, when
In fact, she should be crying but wasn't,
Drowned her in a wash of nasty tears.

*-And do your homework.*
*You need all the schooling you*
*Can get cause sure as shit*
*Your looks ain't paying*
*Nobody's rent.*

## Seven

## Forensics

**Fade out. Dissolve the sound:**

Crushing words
Are better muted.

**Panoramic head spin:**

No one is listening. No one
Is looking in. No one is--

She could die right here
Right now. This very breath
Just in time for dessert.
It's the least she could do.

**Ripple:**

She hangs from thread of

Body bag. A graying blue.
Sounds of dinner conversations
Continue without her.

They are uninterrupted
By porcelain dishes crashing
Soundlessly onto the wooden floor.
Shattered China. Family heirloom.

They are thrift store legacies,
Second hand wounds.

Loud talk walking. Drowning
Out the wails of haunted and
Abandoned dreams.

A gurney carrying her corpse
Slides slowly 'cross dining table.
It is as an ice plow splitting through
A frozen tundra.

Her body is a
Ghost ship no one believes in.
She is captain going down.
It's taco night.

**Zoom in on instructions stitched to toe tag:**

*In the case of suicide always remember*

*It's up the road, not 'cross the street.*
*Do-overs are for losers.*

She ponders the accuracy.

Here's a question. There's the answer.
How common must suicide be to have
Cliches on techniques devoted to
The art of self-extinction?

Very.

**Pan out. Optic left:**

Review escape routes: Emergency exits exist.
Rehearse backup plan: Emergency exits exist.
In case of emergency: Exits exist.

Up the road.
Not 'cross the street.

*But why go solo?*

She is not alone.
Shadows scurry from
Peripheral's domain.

Hold head.
Block out.

Bite tongue.
Go under.

Pull away. Get
Shoved down.
*Wait here.*

*I'll be back.*

She takes familial inventory.
Runs her scars over each relation.
Memories in the form of
Puzzle pieces.

Hover low and over
Until she finds the one
Who fits the wound.

*Yeah, you did this. I
Can smell it. Snake juice
I be juju. Come to getchu.*

This much she knows--
Evidence is for amateurs.
Un-slaughter as you go.

Blood bath soothes
An arid soul. Keep it
Clean. No residue.

No cops. No remorse.

**Dissolve. Zoom in to Headspace (Pan in on checklist):**

**Self:** ~~Un-slit~~
**House:** ~~Un-torched~~
**School:** ~~Un-bombed~~
**Self:** ~~Un-overdosed~~
**Dog:** ~~Un-poisoned~~
**Cat:** ~~Un-microwaved~~
**Self:** ~~Un-hung~~
**Father:** ~~Un-blasted~~
~~By both shotgun and AK?~~
**Self:** ~~Un-drowned~~
**Mother:** ~~Un-bludgeoned~~
**Self:** ~~Un-flung from bridge~~
**Sister:** Un-strangled and untortured-
      *Hmmm, better check on that.*

**Pan to dinner scene as viewed from headspace:**

Conduct visual assessment

Of sister's throat. Right eye
Left cheek. Fingernails
Both hands.

Oh-
And feet.

Don't forget
The feet.

Make sure
Mother isn't
Bleeding.

Evaluate
Father for signs of successful
Un-castrating.

Inhale fully and discretely.
Note any trace of cooked cat
In the air.

*Fetch the girl.*

*Tell her. Say, shhhhh!*
*Tell her. Say I said*
*Be cool.*

*Don't go drawing*
*Attention to us.*

***Act Normal.***

## Eight

## Silent Assassins

But then there are the looks.
The silent assassins holding post
In the crevice of every expression.
Skilled utmost in the finesse of
Felony without substantiation.

Snipers locked and loaded
In the corners of every smile,
Ever present, ever vigilant.

She be three witches slipping
Through grey matter striations.
One eye between them. Us.
Spy everything. Eagle
Bald. Bold and brazen.

Such must guards of
Barless prisons be.

Flashlights banging on cells
Of the sleeping. Occasionally pausing
To rattle. Sometimes stopping
To terrorize.

Such must sentries of
Abandoned kingdoms be.

And hers were infested
With the vested eyes of flies.
And she could see hundreds
By eight at a time.

## Nine

## Cloud Clover

They wanted to cut off her lips.
The rubber ships kept afloat in
The swallow above her throat.
They heard more than they spoke.

If nothing else, she knew
The gossip of ghosts who
Kept watch while she slept.
Billowing. Clouds trembling
With mumble. Clouds.

Weighted with words. Whispers
Skuttling through crevices in cranium.
Skirmishes breakout on the outskirts
Of cerebral cortex. Clouds.

Heaving. Raining down and over
Fields of orchids she has never seen.

Rushing. Rampant through alleyways
She knows too well. Clouds.

Flooding her lungs. She is lost at sea.
Blurred are the shores of her reality. Head inside
A thunderstorm she is scratching at illusions.
Currents pull her under. Drag her over
Pillows wet with weeping. Clouds.

## Ten

# Flicker

She wraps her head to
Cover her ears, lest the murmurs
Get loose and leave her lonely.

They are the only company in this
Gaping solitude. Where suns rise and set
To the soliloquy of a pariah shunned
By all but the whispers.

They are a comfort, though she
Can't quite make them out. They soothe
They are a calm inside a raging storm
Invisible to all but her.

Glitch

There is
A breaking

Happening
Here.


An implosion no one notices.
Including herself. It is a sweet release
She drifts inside the silence of the sound.


Only the ringing in her ears and
The baseline of her heartbeat tells her
She is alive inside the quiet.


Filter


Violet vortex bleeds into view.
Vision is now as an overexposed film
To her underdeveloped reasoning.
Kaleidoscopic striations spin surly.


She is the light at tunnel's end
And yet, she is the tunnel itself.
All matter of travel has been halted
Save for the floats in her parade.


She is smiling. Waving at nothing
In particular. Sliding toward a
Something already in possession
Of her fragile mind.

## Eleven

## Cradled

Then one night, towards middle,
She fell down a sleep without a lock
Or ladder with which to climb

From beneath the breach
And found herself buried beneath
Lifetimes of hateful words.

Insults that stung.
Screams that demolished.
Secrets that stained.
Joke's that bruised far
Beyond the punchlines.

The cruelest,
The utter ugliest, always
From those she loved.

When she finally managed
To dig herself up and out. She ran.
Sprinted with all her strength.

Past the woods where
Her uncles touched her.
Where her aunties let them.
Where her parents made her
Apologize for being violated.

Past the schoolyards
Where the resident bullies
Obliterated her behind buildings,
In circles, in front of audiences
That included her friends.

Past the snake pits of relatives
Who called her slow. Slutty. Stupid
Who laughed when she cried.

Who sneered when she laughed.
Who left when she needed
Them more than breath.

She ran past the dark
And into the dawn. She skipped
'Cross the sun. Crashed up
Through brain matter gasping
For air. Sheets soaked. A stranger

In a strange bed.

## Twelve

## Initiate Precept

The criterion is clear:

Almond eyes; big and bright.
Mascaraed and shadowed. Always.
Not the pitiful beady ones you got
Popped with. No. They have to be
*Almond* eyes. *Those* are beautiful.

Learn the difference between big lips
And full lips. Yours are big. The magazine girl's
Are full. Even the white ones. *They* are
Beautiful.

Perfect skin. No blemishes. None. Ever. Ever
See a pimple on TV? Only in infomercials, right?
And even then, they have the word *'before'* under them.

**Fade to late night infomercial. Embed cheerful Caucasian male narration throughout:**

*This is Jane **before** the Acme Beast Tamer 5000*
*(Insert picture of ugly Jane above the word **'before'**).*
*Notice her blotchy skin. Wow, that's disgusting!*

*Notice how she fades into backgrounds unnoticed.*
*Much like a liquor store sack tumble- weeding*
*Across a ghetto street. Nobody notices Jane*
*Because nobody cares. She's ratchet.*

**Before,** therefore equals Ugly
Simple mathematics: $\mathbf{B+Ug^2}$

Now, ***After*** people are the chosen ones.

*Flawless complexions.*
*Smooth skin. Firm bodied.*
*Not jiggly and dented like yours.*

*Not to mention perfect breast. Perky*
*Some as big as cantaloupes, but perky,*
*Nonetheless. Not at all like the droopy*
*Kiwis you got cursed with.*

*And that forehead--*

*Nothing about you resembles the **After** people*

*It takes money to get to the **After** life, and by*
*The looks of you I'm guessing--*

**Continue infomercial:**

*Join the millions who've been rescued*
*From the pits of obscurity by morphing*
*From uncomely, undesirable, invisible **Befores,***

*Into Irresistible, everybodywantsme **Afters,***
*For just three easy installments of*
*$39.99 + shipping & handling.*

*But wait!*

*If you order within the next 10 minutes*
*And like us on Facebook (Insert photoshopped*
Skinny white girl floating angelic over
The word **After i**n social media profile picture)

*We'll throw in a bucket of*
***G'on Get White** absolutely free!*
*Call now and get like Jane!*

*Notice how she commands admiration*
*Wherever she goes? Much like a goddess*
*But better! She's a supermodel!*

*Of course, you do! Everybody*

*Notices because everybody cares!*
*She's **beautiful!***

**After**, therefore equals Beautiful
$A= [Ug^2 \text{-} Ug^2][BeU(t)x2] + (39.99)3$
+shipping & handling

Offer void where prohibited. Cases shown are atypical. Read the fine print for deception. Side effects include disappointment, delusion, depression, approval dependency, codependent relationships and dreams of suicide because what we're selling is bullshit and your susceptibility to our tactics is directly correlated to the utter lack of self-esteem caused by societal conditioning by way of relentless subliminal messaging made possible by government and corporate funding. Where applicable, seek help.

Cross verify
Show your work
$Ug2\text{-}(\$) = 0 \times BeU(t)$
No remainder

# Thirteen

## Shift

So, when he said it, she turned to see
Who he was talking to. Seeing no one, she
Turned back, and into her very first kiss.

An experience she almost missed entirely
Because of her mind. Her mind. Her mind.
Who did he say was... *beautiful?*

Between the second compliment and
Third kiss, it was beginning to sink in, but still,
She wondered, *who was beautiful*?

By the time he paid her fare and
Stood so she could sit, she thought
She knew but wasn't sure.

By the time he squeezed her thigh
And spun the spell again, she was eye

Deep in bliss and fighting off a scream.

Unhinged. She was a child
On a mach10 roller coaster. Breakneck
Spiraling at hyper speed.

But wanting him to think
She thought such compliments commonplace,
She settled on a smirk.

All the while an echo
Watched the ugly struggle 'gainst
A beautiful death.

It was *her*.
*He* thought *she*
Was beautiful.

*He*. A man.

One of those elusive phantoms
She had been told and so believed
Would never want her for himself,

Thought

*She*. A girl

Who couldn't stand to meet

Her own eyes in the mirror because
The ridicule would surely
Make her cry,

Was...*Beautiful.*

## Fourteen

## Free

By the time they arrived at the motel
She did not remember how they got there.
But she knew one undoubtable thing.

He
Found
Her

*Beautiful.*

Worlds unchained.
Thoughts untethered.
There was no returning
From beauty.

She had heard it.
Beautiful. He said so.

Until now,
She had been invisible.
Until now
She had been anonymous.

Fuck her relations for
Keeping this secret from her.
They hated her. They were jealous.
But she was free now.

She
Was
Free.

Beautifully,
Vibrantly
Free.

A mind. Unleashed
A sleep. Disturbed. Somewhere
A portal is unlocked.

## Fifteen

## Lamb

Somewhere an innocent
Gives her flesh to a power
Larger than herself.

Somewhere, inside a hollow
An altar is being prepared.
Somewhere, inside a darkness
An echo is growing.

A beauty,
Stirring in the dark
Of silence.

Somewhere, a hooded knight
Casts his eyes upon an anima's repose
Begging mercy for a sin he will not
Refrain from committing.

Flesh becomes him. Blood thick
In veins of shaft. And she. A virgin
Come willing to his web of want.

He will have her.
Child, though she is.

He will ravage this tender thing,
Child, though she is.

This sweet young fruit.
Child, though she is.

The vultures will be pleased
With the succulent scraps
He will offer on her behalf.

And still
*-God have mercy*

And still
*-I know I promised*

And still
*-Forgive me*

And still
*(Dam breaks)*

And still
*-I beg you*

And still
*(Rage rushes)*

And still
*-I will have her*

And still
*-absolve me*

Somewhere,
A jonesing god
Grants favor.

For beauty be a
Bounty worthy of he
Who slays the ugly

Somewhere,
She was
*Touched.*

## Sixteen

## Alchemy

There in the convulsion of conjure
An ugly is shifting and on the verge
Of a metamorphosis.

A moth shook of her chrysalis so violently
Her wings become the stained glass
Iridescence of a Monarch's cloak.

Royal, she is, shed of her confines.
The open air rustles her apexes so that she
Lay splayed. The most delicate of creatures.

Overwhelmed by the weight of
Her regal new wings, the butterfly
Lies flightless;

Searching
For God in the clouds

Of a motel sky.

## Seventeen

## Flesh from Shadow

In his mouth, she heaves
In currents of urgency unfathomable.
Pulled under, she is submerged
Inside a sect of selves.

Each sect is a multitude of mirrors
Undulating in rhythm to a distant calling.
Distortions of versions of herself.
Eyes immense, mouths agape.

Some screaming soundlessly.
Others subdued yet beaming. All
Fusions of everyone she has ever known.

They are beckoning her. She is at once
Afraid and curious. There is a light flittering
From an origin she cannot make out.

It pulsates between blinding and
Scarcely discernible. She stills herself
In the strobe, barely breathing.

She is lost in a labyrinth of
Shadows and sounds. A dizzying
Maze of scorn and salvation.

It is here she catches
Glimpse of fleshed shadow.
A mirrored reflection looking
Nothing like her.

The form is older than she, that she can tell.
There is a glimmer in her eyes, the
Kind that hints at something dark
Something disturbed.

She is smiling. A stunningly
Heart-stopping smile that only serves
To race the pulse and dry the mouth.

She has the build of a dancer
Sinewy. Seductive. She stands
Motionless for moments. She is

A shadow
More flesh than shadow.
A shadow

More human than she.

She runs after her, the shadow
Who has now disappeared
Into the sect of mirrors

But the labyrinth spins out of control
A cacophony of chatter and winding tunnels.
She can feel herself begin to fall

Spiraling circles
Into themselves.
Falling. Flailing.
Never landing.

# Eighteen

## Surge

She woke

To a needle,
A feather,
And a rope.

Between her teeth
There lies a note

*-Love Echo*

## Nineteen

## New Eyes

There is no force so powerful
As that with which a sinned against soul
Rises to vindicate itself.

No design as omnipotent
As that with which one shunned
Resolves to prove herself worthy
To eyes blind to all but beauty.

And so, she became
Goddess in the hands of kings.
Stripper on stage before paupers.
Seductress in the gutters of ghouls.

It was there, wrapped in the
Warmth of her creator,
Enveloped by the walls of his
Arms and chest on all sides,

That ugly became merely the
Placenta in which beauty incubated itself
Until born through the sweat and jism
Of a dark knight's transgression.

Her maker's hands expand. Fingers,
Sun rivers rushing over the evolution of
Her new flesh. A dawning. The cosmos in his
Eyes; a fresh kill on his breath.

He is an unwitting co-conspirator
In the creation of an ethos whose
Era has entered the atmosphere.

For in all the realms of
Lowercase gods there is an
Echo for each existence.

And her, formerly invisible,
Ia a force set free, finding delicious her
Beautiful new reality.

## Staccato

By the time he pulled himself
Out of his pants and into her mouth,
An occurrence took place.

She didn't even know his name.
John, did he say? No, Jay. Jason.
It doesn't matter. He. Thinks
She. Is beautiful.

He cannot contain himself.
A blind man can see that she is the
Woman of his dreams. He didn't
Even ask her name. Did he?

By the time he threw her, without regard
Onto cigarette-burn riddled spread, he was
Silent as quicksand before the swallow.

Never uttering another urging word
Neither reaching for condom nor caress
Before bludgeoning a path between
Her still partly blue-jeaned legs.

Which, now that she paid closer attention
Were really rather pretty. The curve of her
Thighs. The silken slopes of her calves.

Yes, this will do quite nicely indeed.
Ripe she is in all her innocence
Never mind the rough embrace.

It is to be expected from a man
So entranced, passion overwhelms him.
And can she blame him?

Take notes

The bend of her toes.
They should be painted.
The decision was made.

After all, she was beautiful now
A woman in love. A whirlwind affair
The man of her fantasies lost in
The bliss between her knees.

She couldn't wait to show him off.

Where would they go afterwards?
Probably to one of restaurants off 7th
The ones with the hosts and valet.
She should have worn a dress.

By the time he collapsed,
Spent and separate from, but
Still inside of her. Lying
Breathless and vacant

A name that was not hers
Slipped out in a sigh that
Slid down her cheek and
Into her mental.

Though she didn't mind the
Salt in the sound or the
Sting of the wet. Not really.

Surely the name belonged
To somebody *After.*
Surely, she reminded him of her
And all things pretty.

Surely, he made her
A woman, beautiful
Like *her.* Whoever
*Her* was.

She was an
**After,** too, now. And
No longer a virgin.

## Twenty One

## The Rebirth

She fell asleep
A new woman in the arms
Of an old man.

Body bruised in hues of blues
From heel to head. Blood dried
And caked between her legs.
She is deep in a dreamscape.

She is floating in a fog over her
Body which is lying in the middle
Of a playground. Her body is bloated.
It is outlined in pink sidewalk chalk.

She wants to get up but can't move.
There are children playing ring-around-the-rosie
Around her corpse. She is naked. They are laughing.
She is dead.

Mind flickers
Like an incandescent bulb
Rattled in the aftermath of a
Fading hurricane.

She floats.

There is a group of boys
Battle rapping in an abandoned building.
One of them bangs his fist on a wall
To make a beat. They take turns
Banging. Banging. Banging.

By the time she woke up naked and
Alone inside a squalid room rented
By the hour, and *only* for the hour,

Or so the throaty voice was shouting
Between slurred curses and doughy fist
Pounding on flytrap feigning door;

She was disoriented
And confused. Should she wait?
Where did he go? Did he leave a note?
Shit, she's supposed to be
Home by now?

Where was she?

She had never been to this part
Of the city before. Was she
even in the city?

She was lost.
Lost, but still
Beautiful. Everything
Was beautiful.

Everywhere he touched.
Echoes and echoes of beauty
Ringing in her ears.

You.
Are.
Beautiful.

He said it.
Didn't he?

Yes. He
Had been
There.

A towering banyan
Among the patches of crabgrass
Dotting her life.

And hers were legs

Jutting. Tender and green
Bold and brilliant from the
Seething cracks in concrete
Breeding ground.

Spreading.
Crawling.
Climbing.
Wrapping.
Holding on.

They had given way to the swell
Of his uprising pushing through the
Stratosphere of her womanhood,
Shaking the earth beneath her
For miles and miles and-

By the time she paid the man
With the sour breath and leering
Eyes for the extra hour

Because, no, she could not
Pay only for the 17 minutes past
That she slept through.

Unless, of course,
She had *other forms* of payment.
*Cause an hour don't make*
*No change.* As he put it.

But she wasn't
Sure about that.
Not at all.

## Twenty Two

## Concerto for One

She was a song, now.
A ballad in purples and blues.

Every bruise
A note played in D Major.
Every tear
A crescendo in B Minor.

Every word a lyric.
Every '*Beautiful*' a chorus.
Every touch a masterpiece

Left by a dark knight.
Blessed by a junkie god
Forgiven by a world
Gone mad.

It is her favorite opus.

It is the score of a woman
Beautiful and bleeding.

It is the theme music
She will step to
Until the end of time .

## Twenty Three

## Circles

By the time she found herself
Finally on the night train heading
Home. She had walked
A dozen blurry blocks.

Looking.
Searching
For him.

Just to make sure
He did, in fact, believe
She was beautiful.

By the time she came upon
The sidewalk leading to her building,
She didn't remember leaving to arrive.

The words he spoke

Awoke in her an
Obsession.

A preoccupation.
To be beautiful, and only beautiful.
Again, and again and-
Was she?

By the time she stood watching the
Blood swirl candy cane cyclones
Down her beautiful new legs through
Cumulus steam of shower

She didn't think to re-collect
The chastity she lost along
The long way home.

She was bewildered.
Falling autumn leaves
Crimson and gold

Twisting through thoughts
Of a man who thought
Her beautiful.

She was grateful
For the hickies he left. Sacred poems
Across her breast.

She would show them off as
Proof of her beautiful new existence
Should the vultures at school try to
Tear off her pretty new wings
And force her to slither, again,
through the ugly mud.

And they would,
Force her down on her knees,
Make her regret having had
A good thing.

For having the audacity
To flaunt it. Like a crown
Among peasants.

They would make her crawl.
They would shove her face in the dirt.
They would make it hurt.

A reminder of who she was.
Of where she came from.
Of what she'd always be.

By the time she
Skipped school the
Next morning
She was chasing
The sounds of the ether.

Apparitions visible
And not.

## Twenty Four

## The Killing Yields

She was a full six blocks into her search
By the time her schoolmates sat tossing
Mind grenades, expertly over 2% and
Chili dogs in the cafeteria.

*-Uh uh, did you see the new girl?*
*-Girl, yes. Got a face like a pug dog.*
*Lips and all, damn shame*

*-Bitch could at least get herself some weave*
*Shit, they got a sale goin' on at the Korean store.*
*Buy one get one free, ol' broke ass.*

*-Ain't no reason for folk to be goin' round*
*Looking like Thelma from Good Times with*
*That played out afro. Naps ain't for everybody.*
*She needs to perm that shit.*

*Then had the nerve not to*
*Speak to nobody. Carryin' herself*
*Like she Queen of Da Nieyo*
*Or some shit.*

-The Nile.

-*What?*

-It's a river. In Egypt
You remedial trick
And it's called- The Nile.

(Positioning)

-*What the fuck?*
*Da Nieyo, the Nile*
*Same shit, bitch.*
*Ain't nobody ask for no*
*Geometry lesson!*

-It's Geography
You ignorant bitch.
Damn!

(Pull Down)

-*Yeah ok, again with the big words*
*You think cuz you read a fuckin' book*

*Your ass is getting out the hood.*
*Too funny.*

*-What the fuck good it do*
*Pronouncin' some shit you*
*Ain't never gonna see?*

*Read on, you bougie bitch.*
*You be the only genius rockin'*
*Name tags and aprons. Right*
*Up the street. Like everybody else.*

*Talkin' bout-*
*Welcome to Hood Burger*
*Can I take your order?*
*You want that*
***Nile** sized?*

-All laugh but one

(Escape Maneuver)

-You know what? Fuck you
And your ghetto ass mentality.
You are one fucked up bitch,
I see that now.

Your punk ass is scared as hell
Of being left behind. All by yourself in

this motherfucker, ol' lonely ass.

Waiting on your welfare
Check and watchin' Maury
You fuckin' loser.

Don't worry, though. I'll come see you
On the regular, ok? Every time I need
My windows washed at the stoplight.

(The truth)

*-Bitch, I'll kill you!*

-Not if I kill you first, you
Sorry piece of shit!

(The ugly truth)

*-Both you bitches need to shut the hell up*
*And pass the goddamn soy sauce. All I know is*
*I am sick! Of ramen noodles,*
*And that's real.*

*Like we ain't got enough enemies without*
*Makin' war with each other, and shit. That's*
*Why we gonna always be at the bottom of*
*Every damn thing. Every goddamn time.*
*Niggas make me sick.*

*I need some Black folk in my life.*
*That's word.*

## Twenty Five

## Heard

Words.
She needed
Words.

By the time she'd ordered
Her third chocolate shake, she'd cried
For the fourth time in two hours.

*Maybe he hadn't said it.*

No, but she heard him. Yes.
Maybe he didn't mean it. No.
He meant it.

*God, please
Let him have
Meant it.*

She couldn't be wrong.
Couldn't let herself think beyond
The questions to the answers.

She had had enough of ugly,
She wanted to be beautiful.

Where was he?
She was beautiful
Remember?
She forgot.

By the time she
Swapped her chocolate shakes
For bottles of hard cider, she had
Given up on finding him.

The one and only human being
In this entire wide and fucked up world
Who saw her for who she was.

He
Saw
Her.

She
Heard him
See her.

Him

Who found her so seductive
He made himself her first and
Then got lost.

That's how beautiful she was.
He said so. And now she couldn't
Remember his name.

She had to find him.
Had to hear those words.
Her life depended on it.

Jonathan, right?
No, Joe. Maybe.
Was it a *J* at all?

Mark? No. Hell no
Definitely began with a J
Like joy.

## Twenty Six

## Nobody's Rent

By the time she convinced herself
That the reason for her memory loss
Was because *she* did not care and not
Because he never told her,

She was studying for final exams in
A sunlit corner of the public library.
Being as she wasn't sure if she was
In fact, beautiful

She thought it a good idea to
Heed her mother's advice in the event
That her looks were proven to be, alas
Worthless in rental agreements.

By the time he seated himself
On the chair opposite her at the table
She had already noticed him notice her.

A skill in which she had become
Remarkably acute since that day with Jeremy
No, Jerome. Jack? Fuck it.

Exigency lingered, ever-present
An itch in demand of a fix. Needing
To see again, the eyes that said
What the lips would not.

And she saw them.
Here and there.
Now and then.

And whenever she saw them
She would allow them to approach
Just close enough to feel the words.

And she felt them.
Now and then.
Here and there.

Seldom ever from the same pair of eyes.
Seldom ever for very long. Always there was
A price to pay. A piece of herself to swap

In the exchanges
That never lasted
Long enough.

Usually just long enough
To make her believe it real before
Reminding her it was not.

Sometimes just
Long enough to send
Her to the clinic.

Once so long
She had to have it
Aborted.

## Twenty Seven

## Words

Words.

She needed words.
The balm for wounds
Old and new. So few

Have mastered
Application of
The verbiage.

For it is not
So much the words
Themselves.

Rather the vibratory
Inflections. Wordless sonnets
Passed through air.

How the sound curls
Like smoke of incense
Slid over eardrums.

How energy wraps
Around waist. Awakening
Pearl from slumber.

Tender is the tenor
In symphony's caress.
Dulce is the honeyed tongue.

The sweeter the lie the
The deeper the truth.

It was, too, the unspoken
The nuance of a glance held only
Long enough to invite.

It was the glimmer in
The eyes. The glow in
Windowed souls.

She has heard it told
That the eyes don't lie.
But we know better.

The eyes seduce.
The gaze compels.

The brow beckons.
The purity traps.

It is the spirit in the verbs

It is the bravado
It is the humility
It is the aggression
It is the timidity

It is all of it, yes
And then the words

Words

That make scars disappear behind
Flawless smile of a ghetto goddess.

Words

That make fat girls voluptuous
In succulent seduction. They fall soft
As satin in sway of lover's hands.

Words

That make flat breasts full
As harvest moons over sea
Of breath and bliss, bound to

Bottoms of intoxication.

Words

That make nappy hair magnificent
Through fingers reaching ever for stars
Above the grasp of dreams.

Words

That make big lips full. Sensuous
Temptations sweet as candied sin
On tongued salvation.

Words

That make beady eyes almond round
And bright as phoenix sky. So clear they are,
The night wind prays they never cry again.

Words

That lived this very moment
Within the purity in the suave facade
Of the smiling boy before her.

## Twenty Eight

## The Moments

She lived for these moments
These transactions of glances
Promising validation.

The weaving wisps of words
Warming worlds orbiting away
From undertow of soul's reflection.

They hold within their sing-song serenade
The dust in which angels fly sky. High.

And if body and soul be sold for this
Ephemeral anesthesia, of mind succumb
To spiral spin through spirit's ugly lonely.

So be it.

If to be held in flicker of the moment,

Pulsating Polaroid in strobe of shattered
Prism, means falling through wish thick
Abyss slick with mists of kisses, then
Wishes exist and she will be held at all.

So be it.

Should eye have mercy and heart have faith
Then ear will hear when whispers wind of all so right
And righteous in dimming light of mind's recall

So be it.

She is beggar shaking cup
In crowded corners of the dreams
Who come and go, but never stay

Whose change is but an hour.
Shower her with charity
And make it worth her while.

So be it.

# Twenty Nine

## Fracture

*To be held at all.*
*They never hold you.*
*Not once they have had*
*Their way with you.*

*Not for very long, anyway.*
*The girl gets low sometimes*
*That's when I step in. Or*
*Should I say, come out?*

*She needs love.*
*Out here in these streets,*
*Everybody needs*
*Love, right?*

*So that's what I do.*
*I go lookin' for love. Keep*
*The child from killin' herself.*

*Her folks ain't never gave a shit.*
*Always favored the other girl*
*But I like this one.*

*She sweet. A little too sweet sometimes*
*But stickin' with me, we make it through.*
*Don't need nobody between us.*

*There was one boy, besides the first*
*Had her caught up in the chaos of her emotions*
*Ended up leaving her without a word or whistle*
*Broke her heart. I had to teach him a lesson.*

*Took him to the backseat.*
*Him, her, and me. Had ourselves a real*
*Good time. Last good time he ever had.*
*Nobody fucks with my girl.*

*Who me? Shit,*
*Can't Nobody hurt me, baby.*
*Even if I wanted 'em to.*
*It's just the way it is.*

*I can't feel a damn thing.*
*That's why I came for the girl.*
*She feels too much.*

*That ain't good.*

*Not in this world.*
*Not in the next either.*

*But here's the thing,*
*I ain't good at finding*
*That Forever Love.*

*The kind of love make you*
*Find a home in your own Self. The kind that make*
*Your soul come to the party.*

*Say, this is me and*
*Everything I got is yours*
*To hold and behold.*

*The kind of love make you*
*Wanna take your heart out your chest*
*And offer it up for safekeeping*

*Is it out there for us?*
*Fuck if I know. For now, I take*
*What we can get. That high. That*
*Drug. That Beautiful chase.*

*Though, I admit,*
*It never holds the magic*
*Of the first time.*
*But it'll do.*

*It gets us through and*
*I ain't gotta worry 'bout whether not*
*We waking up in the mornin'.*

*But*
*That first*
*Time*

*Never*
*As good as the*
*First time*

*Yeah,*
*That first*
*Time.*

## Thirty

## Clarity

Free fall into focus.
The moment is not random
It is providence.

Here. It happened right here. Here.
Hear. Heard. I. You. Lied to me. It hurt.
I was hurt and it was you who hurt me.

I do not forgive you.

You were my first.
First lie. First kiss.
First hope. First wish.
First fuck. First thirst.
Last first.

I was a virgin then.

And then you spoke
In talk so pretty I forgot your name.
Do, love, lie again.

The first time was so beautiful
The ugly died and I was born.
Remember? I do.

It was you. I remember your eyes
But not your name. Don't be angry.
I didn't mean to demean you the way you
Demeaned me, I mean, I wanted to

But couldn't. You were God to me.
You knew everything, yes, everything.
Including my thoughts.

You fingered my mind like
The pages of a glossy magazine.

I was stranded in the abandoned
Projects of the classifieds, hitchhiking
My way to the glamorous life
On the front page.

Oh, I knew I would not belong there
An ugly hag among the beauty queens,
But a girl can dream. And I did.
I dreamed.

I was a cover girl accidentally
Existing in barren gutter of the
Classifieds. I was trying so hard
To get out of there, but she was
Always getting in the way.

It was you.
Reader of mind with gaze clairvoyant as x-ray.

It was you.
Wielder of wands and magic words and spells.

It was you.
Who unraveled the world as I knew it and spilled the se-
crets.

It was you.
Who walked up to me and made the ground fall away.

I was *before*
You were the path leading to
The *after* life

You were perfect
And in your perfection, you
Demanded your reflection
Look like you; no matter who it was
Who was not you, because

They were them, not you.

You were omnipresent sentry
Of beauty's presentation. You were
Beautiful and she was ugly

So, you killed her
And made me
Beautiful. Like you.

You were everywhere
And everyone around me.
In you, I saw my very self
In mystic stranger on the corner.

In you, I heard the one and only
Friend I never had.
Don't tell my enemies
It will only hurt their feelings.

In you, I finally felt my father's love for me.
You must've stolen, I thought because he never
Had it to give. Not even when he wanted to.

In you, the words my mother seldom spoke
Swelled like oceans, settling like so many
Treasure chests of talks we never opened.

In you, I had protective love

Of sister's loyal alliance,
Absent in blood relation
Since separation
From the womb.

You were the boy who always
Looked but never spoke, finally smiling
Your embrace and hand in courtship.

You were devilish grin
Of schoolgirl gossip
Wiping itself away to make
Room for me at coveted table.

In you was every joy not mine to have.
You found me in the street without a soul
And took me in. You stroked my fur and
Fed me spoiled milk and fresh ground glass
From paper bowl.

Even my purr was pretty in your touch.

You were no one and nowhere
At all times. You were fragmented
Figment of delirium's daydream.

You were oasis in wasteland and
Just as I imagined, I had only imagined.
But even imagined, I needed you.

You were my sixty minutes in the prison yard
Running wildly away from twenty-three-hour stints
Lashing holes into the feathers on my back.

You were good and evil sharing studio space
In an eastside sublet in spirit. You were angel.
You were demon. You were roommates
Without cable and nothing better to do.

You were each holding a breast in one hand
And speaking in dialects so ancient, I could only
Translate them through the drums in my ears.

Angelic demon, you were incubus in flesh
Snapping through ribs to resuscitate my failing heart.
    Angel wanting only that I should know of life and all alive
with living.
    Demon's only thought, clever, better ways to kill and then
revive.

You were both. You were neither. Which explains
How you could speak the words of healing god
Mending bruise and brokenness.

But only for the moment, it's... a fact.

For the moment tender mending was completed,
Entered you, unholy guardian, finding delicious,

The deliberate fucking of my selves into
Incoherent rhetoric of tongues.

My love the shards of glass
You ground to dust and fed to
me from paper bowl. Purring
All the while until I fell asleep
To your roaring lullaby.

You left before I knew your name
Scrolling love notes crimson purple to the
Breaking heart inside my chest.

For you
There are no
Words.

## Thirty One

## Continuum

But pain. Pain is still a word.
Like- free. Like- me. Like- set.
Like- love. Like- please. Like
Please. Love. Set. Me. Free.

And speak.

Speak it slowly
Say it sweet. But do, Love
Talk to me.

It's easy. See me?
No strings, baby. Just words.
I promise.

Just three. Just, please.
Just close your eyes and speak,
Love. Talk to me.

Weave for me
Those pretty words that
Rouse the soul in me.

That shake the dust
From off these wings and
Shine them opalescent
In the witching hour.

For you be sorcerer
In broad of day. Cast your spell and
Conjure me from tip of tongue

Let it be so.

## Thirty Two

## Ritual

So, by the time he said hello,
This stranger with the blotchy
Skin and pretty teeth.

Manchild wild with decorum
Posturing princedom, she watched
With abject tranced affection.

This spider spinning captivating
Web of conversation for moth with
No intention of escape.

Eyes speaking magic,
Tongue licking puddles
In the hills beneath her blouse.

His voice a familiar
Dank motel.

His smile a
Stinging shower.

Hand's anticipation stroking bowl
From crumpled pages,
To sounds of purrs
Already building
On her tongue.

They were strangers
Separated by books and fables,
But already she could feel

The old acquaintance
In warmth of rhythmic
Words

Hard and thick
Against the glassy splinters
In her throat.

The face is different. The face
Is never the same. And the names.
The names always change. But the hour.
The hour remains.

The hour she knows by heart.

# Thirty Three

## Echo

She, who knows of places
Where ugly goes to die.
Where worlds and words
Are washed away in whirl
Of motel lullaby.

She, who waits
Quietly as promised danger
Smiling shy reciprocation.

The storm in her skirt and
Clouds in her eyes. The smell of
Thunder in her hair the only signal.

*The beggar shakes her cup.*

While minute fondles moment
For pocket change enough for hour

She waits patiently as Deja vu

For him
To make her
Beautiful.

A native of the islands of Hawaii, Journey is a daughter of Lili'uokalani; she is a daughter of Harriet Tubman. Both their lives can be found in the bold pain, rage, resiliency, and strength of her words. Her experience of spending twenty years on and off spoken word stages shines through in the rhythm of her writing style. A recluse by nature, her work is quiet and calculating. She is an observer. She is an investigator. A reporter. A griot.

**Journey Johnson**
*Photo Credit: Kim Roseberry*